ORCHARD BOOKS

96 Leonard Street, London EC2A 4XD

Hachette Children's Books

Level 17/207 Kent Street, Sydney NSW 2000

ISBN 1 84616 048 0

This edition first published in Great Britain in 2005

This edition © Orchard Books 2005

Text and illustrations © individual authors and illustrators; see acknowledgements

The authors and illustrators have asserted their rights

under the Copyright, Designs and Patents Act, 1988.

A CIP catalogue record for this book is available from the British Library.

10 9 8 7 6 5 4 3 2 1

Printed in Singapore

MAGICAL
PRINCESS
STORIES

ORCHARD BOOKS

CONTENTS

THE SLEEPING BEAUTY

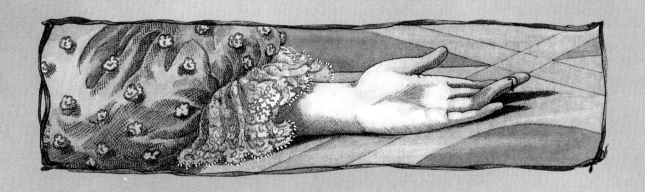

GERALDINE MCCAUGHREAN

ANGELA BARRETT

A BABY DAUGHTER WAS ONCE BORN to a king and queen. She was more beautiful than most, more happy than many, more loved than all but you. Her mother and father wanted her to have everything in life, and what was there to prevent it? They were rich, lived in a splendid palace, and numbered among their friends all the fairies of the forest and field. Fairies with rainbow wings and dresses of gossamer danced at the christening, when the baby was named Aurora, 'the dawn', because she seemed like a promise of a wonderful day to come.

Well, in fact, one fairy was missing, but then Carabosse had disappeared from the country in a huff of temper and a puff of smoke, and had not been seen for years.

So the fairies danced around the cradle like wisps of colour weaving themselves into a rainbow. And they laid their wands on the sleeping child and blessed her with Beauty, Wealth, Joy, Love and Grace.

"And I have a present for her too!" cried a voice.

It was the Fairy Carabosse, quite scarlet with fury, her wings trembling with rage. "Here, Princess," she sneered, tossing like a curse a glittering gift into the cradle. "One day, show what promise you may, win what hearts you might, let *that* be the death of you! Prick your finger and die!"

The other fairies snatched the golden spindle out of the crib, as though it were a poisonous snake. They hurled it out of the window. They begged Carabosse to take back her fearful curse. But the evil-tempered, proud fairy was so offended at having been forgotten, overlooked, that no amount of tears could move her to pity.

"Then I must undo your mischief!" cried the Lilac Fairy, flittering from behind a curtain. "You thought your wicked gift was the last, but I still have mine to give! And though I can't undo your cruel magic, I can blunt its spiteful point. Let the princess not die when she pricks her finger; let her sleep for a hundred years. Then, while she sleeps, let her blessings grow, so that she wakes to yet more joy than her friends can wish her today!"

Carabosse fumed and seethed. She stormed out, slamming the great doors with a noise that shook the very stones of the palace and the very hearts of the guests. But she was no sooner gone than she was forgotten, for the world has no wish to remember the wicked, only the good and the lovely.

Even so, King Floristan banished all spindles and spinning wheels from his kingdom, to make sure Princess Aurora could never prick her finger on one.

In the space of sixteen years, Aurora grew into such a princess as fairy tales are made of. She was beautiful and kind, loved by everyone she met, the pride of her tutors and the joy of her friends. When she danced, the flowers reached higher out of the ground to peep in at the windows.

Princes travelled from all over the world, half in love with the thought of her, instantly in love at the sight of her. At her sixteenth birthday party, four princes presented their compliments to King Floristan and begged for the hand of Princess Aurora in marriage.

"You must ask her yourselves," said her parents. "We wouldn't choose to part with her for all the world, but it is time she spread happiness beyond the bounds of this small kingdom, and enjoyed the happiness of married life as well."

So the Prince of England and the Prince of Spain and the Prince of India and the Prince of France bowed low to the Princess Aurora and partnered her in the dancing. Each one thought he had won her heart.

"She smiled such a smile at me!"

"She held my hand so tenderly!"

"She danced as though her heart was on fire!"

"She laughed at *all* my jokes!"

And yet it was just Aurora's nature to make her friends and guests feel welcome. She was overbrimming with love – but not for any one man more than another.

So it was that she greeted the strange old woman shrouded in grey and cradling something in her arms. "A birthday present for you, my dear," croaked the old crone.

"Do I know you? How very kind. Everyone has been so kind to me today," said Aurora. "What is it?"

About the size of a newborn baby, and almost as light,

it was wrapped in cloth as black as spite. But as Aurora unwrapped it, the present glittered with the yellow of gold, the spangle of fleecy golden yarn, the silver sliver of a sharp needle. It was a spindle for spinning wool into yarn.

"Aurora, don't touch it!" cried her mother.

"Ow! Look, I've pricked my finger. You'd best take it from me. I shall put blood on the pretty wool."

Suddenly the room began to swim and melt, the floor to heave and the ceiling to bow.

"So tired," said Aurora, then fell flat, so deeply asleep that she did not even put out her hands to stop herself from falling.

"Carabosse, your spite has made you the shame of Fairyland. No tongue will ever speak to you again. No face will ever smile your way. Leave here for ever." For a moment, Carabosse stood face to face with the Lilac Fairy, then, with a furious stamp of her foot, she was gone.

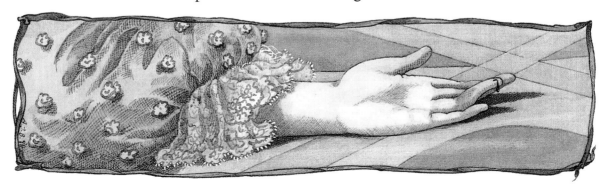

The king and queen were sobbing; the princes had all drawn their swords; Aurora's friends leaned over her, powerless to wake her. "Carry her to her bed!" commanded the Lilac Fairy. "Have you forgotten her fate? To sleep for one hundred years?"

"Then she might just as well be dead, for we shall never see her dance or smile again," sobbed the king. "We shall all be dead long since when she opens her eyes again."

But it was not the Lilac Fairy's intention to keep only Aurora safe, swaddled in dreamless sleep. She swept her wand over the heads of the courtiers and ladies-in-waiting, the princes and guests, the king and queen. And one by one they fell asleep where they stood or sat or sprawled or knelt, sinking into sleep like the leaves settling to the ground from an autumn tree.

And as the Court of King Floristan sank down, up sprang a hedge round his palace; trees and brambles and briars and bushes conjured out of the ground by the Lilac Fairy's wand.

They buried the palace steps, they smothered the palace windows, they muffled its high turrets. The topmost branches stretched protective twigs over the tiled roofs, so that the entire building was smothered in creepers and thorns. So dense was the greenery that a stranger riding by might see no palace there at all.

Of course the people who lived in the villages near by knew of the palace, knew that their king and queen and princess were lost somewhere inside the magic barricade of trees. At first they talked of nothing else. The wonder of it filled their every thought. They tried to get in – failed every time – said the thorns were sharp as needles, the creepers unbreakable.

But there were pigs to feed, the corn to be cut, the sheep to shear, the roof to patch. And people forget the most marvellous things after a few busy years. Those who had ever seen King Floristan, his courtiers and his lovely daughter grew old and died.

After sixty or seventy years the palace in the wood was only a rumour, a legend, a fairy story half believed, about a sleeping beauty and a magic spell.

Exactly one hundred years after Aurora's sixteenth birthday, a young prince called Charmant rode by on the highway with his friends. The forest seemed a pleasant place for a picnic. There was a sudden flicker of movement among the trees.

"A deer!" cried the prince's aide. "Let's hunt it!"

The others were eager enough, but somehow Prince Charmant had no taste for the hunt. When his friends all rushed away into the tangled undergrowth, he remained behind. "What is this place?" he wanted to know. "Why does it give me such a strange feeling? Why does it make my heart beat faster?"

"They say there is a palace in the heart of the forest," said a voice.

"Who are you? Where did you come from? I didn't see you before."

"And at the heart of the palace a room," said the girl in the lilac dress. "And at the heart of the room a bed."

"And at the heart of the bed?"

"A beautiful princess. Sleeping."

The prince leapt up and rushed at the wall of dense green: knotted creepers, tangles of thorn, fallen branches, barricades of tree trunks and, underfoot, slippery moss. "Do you know these parts? Can you show me a way through? Is there a way through?" he begged to know.

"For you? Oh yes. I believe so," said the girl in lilac, and idly breaking off a wand of grass crowned with a star of thistledown she began to pick her way through the tangled undergrowth.

Charmant kept close, following in her footsteps. And strangely enough, the thorns (though they were sharp as needles) never once snagged her lilac dress, nor scratched his own face or hands.

Suddenly his boots stumbled against steps, steps rising upwards to the mossy splendour of an arched doorway. No lock kept him out. No guard challenged him. All the candles had burned down to their holders. All the firegrates were snowy with ash.

In every doorway, passageway and chair, people lay fast asleep. But the girl in lilac did not seem to think them important, for she led him onwards to a bedroom in the heart of the palace. There, in the heart of a snowy bed, untouched by cobwebs, lay a young girl. She was dressed in her finest clothes, as if for a party, and her beautiful face was tilted upwards as if awaiting a kiss.

Strange, to kiss a stranger, especially a stranger lying unconscious in an enchanted palace. And yet he could not help it. It seemed as if Charmant's whole life had been one long wait for this particular day, for this particular kiss.

As their lips touched, her eyes flew open, and his fate was sealed. Beautiful in her sleep, his Sleeping Beauty was still more lovely half awake.

She stirred. She sat up. She put her feet gingerly to the ground and looked around, puzzled at finding herself so far from the party. And yet she did not look around as much as she might, for she could hardly bear to look away from the face of Prince Charmant. Had he kissed her? What a saucy liberty to take, uninvited! And yet she thought her heart would burst if he did not kiss her again.

Throughout the palace, courtiers and ladies-in-waiting stretched and yawned, rubbed stiff necks, puzzled at how they could possibly have fallen asleep at the height of the birthday party. Then they remembered. The king and queen hugged one another as they remembered. It was a strange feeling to go to sleep and wake up one hundred years later.

"Am I old and hideous?" asked the queen.

"Not a day older . . . than . . . than when I last saw you," said the king. "Not one hour. Not one minute."

The orchestra began to pluck their instruments – and found them still in tune, even after a century's silence.

The spell was broken. The trees melted away from round the palace like clematis dying back for the winter months. The thorns melted like spiky frost. The dense leaves flew away like a flock of a million green birds, into a cloudless sky.

All the fairies in Fairyland were invited to the wedding, just as they had been to the christening. Even Carabosse was invited, to see how her evil had been turned to good. But though a herald searched the whole kingdom and far beyond, there was no trace of Carabosse – only a few bitter aloes growing where her gossamer hammock had once hung.

And what more natural at a wedding blessed by fairies, than that the characters of fairy tales should come along as guests: Tom Thumb, Puss in Boots, Red Riding Hood, Beauty and her Beast.

After the ceremony and the dancing, these famous celebrities told their stories as the new candles glimmered in a thousand candelabras, and the wedding guests listened, entranced. Only Aurora and her Prince Charmant remained dancing, held in Love's spell for evermore.

THE
NAUGHTY PRINCESS
AND THE FROG

SAVIOUR PIROTTA

EMMA CHICHESTER CLARK

✳ ✳ ✳ ✳ ✳ ✳ ✳ ✳ ✳ ✳ ✳ ✳ ✳ ✳

Long ago, when wishing could still make dreams come true, there was a king who had many daughters. They were all pretty but the youngest was so beautiful, she even dazzled the sun.

Sometimes, when the weather was warm, the princess went out in the forest and sat by a cool, deep well. One day, she was playing with her favourite golden ball when, all of a sudden, it slipped out of her hands and sank into the water. The princess tried to fish it out but it was no use. The well was much too deep.

"Oh dear," said the beautiful princess, and she started to wail and cry.

"Whatever is the matter?" croaked a voice behind her.

The princess turned to see a huge frog with a wrinkled neck and bulging eyes. "I have dropped my favourite golden ball in the well," she sniffed. "I'd give anything to get it back. Anything."

"Anything?" echoed the frog, hopping into the water.

"Simply anything," repeated the princess. "I'd give my clothes, my jewels, and even my precious crown. It has twelve diamonds in it."

"I have no use for crowns or jewels," said the frog, "but if you promise to let me come and live with you in your palace, if you say I can eat from your golden plate and sleep on your silken pillow, I'll fetch your ball for you."

"What a fool this frog is," thought the princess. "Frogs can only survive near ponds and wells; they can't live with people in houses or palaces." So she smiled and promised the frog she would take him to the palace with her if he retrieved her ball.

The frog promptly dived down to the bottom of the well and, a minute or two later, he surfaced with the golden ball in his mouth.

"Thank you," said the princess. She reached out, took the ball from him and started running away.

"Wait for me," cried the frog. "Don't you remember your promise?"

But the princess took no heed of his words. She just kept on running and running until she reached her father's palace.

The next day, while the princess was having dinner with her father, something came creeping up the marble stairs, going plip, plop, plip, plop, plip. When it reached the top, there was a knock at the door and a croaky voice called, "Princess, Princess, let me in."

"That must be one of your friends come to visit," said her father the king. "Go and open the door."

The princess did as she was told and, to her horror, she saw the frog sitting on the marble doorstep. Bang!

The princess slammed the door shut in his face and returned to the table.

"You are trembling," said her father. "Was there a giant out there?"

"No," said the princess, "it was only a frog." And she told her father about the golden ball and how the frog had retrieved it for her.

Just then the frog knocked on the door again. This time he chanted:

> *"Youngest daughter of the king,*
> *Open up and let me in.*
> *Don't you know what yesterday*
> *You said to me down near the well?*
> *Youngest daughter of the king,*
> *Open up and keep your word."*

"A princess should always keep her promise," agreed the king. "Let the frog in and give him some dinner."

So the princess opened the door again and the frog followed her in, along the hall, across the throne room and into the dining room.

"Lift me up beside you, Princess," he commanded.

Reluctantly, the princess put him on a chair beside her.

"I cannot reach your plate from here," complained the frog. "Put me on the table."

Trying hard not to grimace, the princess put the frog on the table, but as far away from her as possible.

"Bring your plate closer, so we can sup together," said the frog. He licked at her food with his tongue and drank milk from her goblet. The princess was so disgusted that she could hardly touch anything. At last the frog said, "Thank you for that excellent meal. Now take me upstairs to your bed that I might have some sleep."

When the princess heard this, she began to cry. But her father grew angry and said, "You should be grateful to anyone who's helped you in your hour of need. Take the frog

up to your room and let him sleep in peace."

The princess picked up the frog with two fingers and, holding him at arm's length, took him up to her bedroom. There she put him down in a corner, hidden behind a pitcher.

The frog said, "It's not fair that you should lie in a warm bed while I have to make do with a cold, stone floor. Let me sleep on your pillow."

Very reluctantly, the princess lifted the frog on to her soft pillow.

"Now give me a kiss," said the frog.

The princess was horrified. "Do not be impertinent," she cried, "or I shall call my guards and ask them to crush you underfoot."

"If you do not kiss me," said the frog, "I shall tell the king. He won't be pleased when I say you have gone back on your word."

Not wanting to get into further trouble with her father, the princess agreed to kiss the frog. Slowly she bent forward and touched her warm lips to his slimy, cold ones.

All at once, there was a blinding flash of light, and the frog turned into a prince. He was so charming and handsome that the princess was terribly ashamed she'd been so unkind to him and begged his forgiveness. The prince told her how a horrible witch had put a curse on him and how she, the princess, had broken the curse with her kiss.

At dawn a beautiful carriage came to fetch the prince to his kingdom. It was very grand, all made of filigreed gold and drawn by eight strong horses with flowing manes and swishing tails. At the rear stood Faithful Henry, the prince's most loyal servant.

Poor Henry had been very upset when the witch turned his prince into a frog, so the doctor had put three iron bands around his heart to keep it from breaking with sorrow.

The princess asked her father if she might marry the prince, and he consented. So the coach driver cracked his whip and the servants cheered as the coach set off down the street, with Faithful Henry standing in his place at the rear.

When the coach was some distance from the palace, the prince heard a loud crack.

"Henry," he called, "is the carriage falling apart?"

"No, Your Majesty," replied Henry, "it is not the carriage that's breaking, it's one of the iron bands around my heart."

There was another crack, and another. Henry yelled with joy, for at last all three bands had fallen from his heart. Now he was free to celebrate the return of his prince and to take part in the wedding festivities as his master married the beautiful princess.

SNOW WHITE

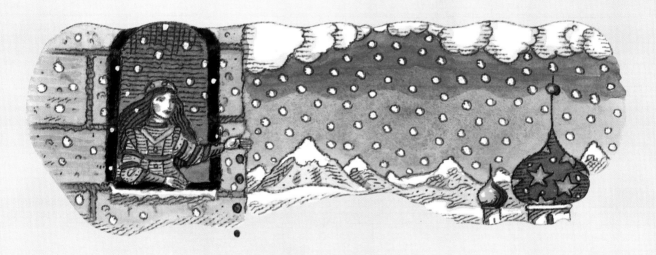

ROSE IMPEY

IAN BECK

✳ ✳ ✳ ✳ ✳ ✳ ✳ ✳ ✳ ✳ ✳ ✳ ✳

I T WAS THE MIDDLE OF WINTER, a long time ago, and a young queen sat sewing by an open window. As she looked up, watching the snow fall like feathers from the sky, she pricked herself, and three drops of blood fell from her finger. The red of her blood, on the white of the snow, framed by the black of the window, was so striking that the queen made a wish that she would have a child as white as snow, as red as blood and as black as the ebony wood of the window frame.

And in time her wish came true; she gave birth to a little girl with snow-white skin, blood-red lips and hair as black as ebony, and they named her Snow White. But when the child was born the young queen died, so joy and sorrow cancelled each other out.

In less than a year the king took a second wife, as beautiful as the first – no, even more beautiful. But she was so vain. The only way she could be happy was in knowing that she was the most beautiful woman in the kingdom.

Now, how could she know this? Because she had a magic mirror, and whenever she stood in front of it she said,

> *"Mirror, mirror, on the wall,*
> *Who is the fairest one of all?"*

And the mirror answered,

> *"Queen, you are the fairest one of all."*

Then she was happy because she knew that the mirror always told the truth.

But nothing stays the same. The years passed and Snow White grew more and more beautiful, as sweet and fresh as the air on a spring morning, and how could the queen compete with that?

The day came when she stood in front of her mirror and asked,

> "Mirror, mirror, on the wall,
> Who is the fairest one of all?"

And the mirror answered,

> "Queen, you were the fairest, 'tis true,
> But Snow White's a thousand times lovelier than you."

From that moment on, every time the queen looked at Snow White she resented her more. And the resentment turned into hatred which soon had the queen in its power. She couldn't rest until she was rid of the girl, so she called her huntsman to her and said, "Take Snow White into the deepest wood and kill her. I never want to set eyes on her again." And, because she wanted to be sure he had done it, she told him to bring back Snow White's heart.

The huntsman was honest and loyal to the queen, but he couldn't bear to think of killing the girl. When Snow White begged him to spare her life he was glad to do it. He knew she wouldn't survive in the woods for long, without food or shelter, but at least his own conscience would be clear.

To satisfy the queen, the huntsman captured a wild boar and took back its heart and the wicked woman ate it, thinking that she was devouring her enemy. That's how much she hated Snow White.

Meanwhile Snow White hurried ever deeper into the wood. By evening, she was completely lost.

At last she came to a cottage. Inside everything was neat and welcoming. A table with a snow-white cloth was set for seven people, food and drink already waiting at each place. And along one wall were seven little beds, covered with snow-white quilts. By now Snow White was so hungry and so tired that she couldn't resist taking just a mouthful from each plate and a sip from each cup.

Then she tried to decide which bed to lie on. But each bed in turn was unsuitable: it was either too long or too short, too high or too low, too hard or too soft, until she tried the seventh bed, which was just right. She lay down on it and fell asleep, safe at last.

Some time later the owners of the house returned, seven dwarfs who worked all day mining for gold in the mountains. They could soon tell that they had had a visitor; things weren't exactly as they'd left them.

"Someone's been sitting on my chair," said the first.

"Someone's been eating my food," said the second.

"Someone's been drinking my wine," said the third.

"Someone's been using my knife," said the fourth.

"And my fork," said the fifth.

"And my spoon," said the sixth.

"Someone's been meddling with my things too," said the seventh.

Then the first dwarf noticed that someone had been lying on his bed, because the quilt was creased. Soon each of them found that his quilt had been lain on. But the seventh found that his was *still* being lain on. There was Snow White fast asleep on his bed.

The other dwarfs crowded around her. She looked so sweet and comfortable that they hadn't the heart to disturb her. They left her to sleep in peace, and the seventh dwarf spent an hour with each of the others throughout the night.

In the morning, when Snow White woke, she was afraid, but the dwarfs soon reassured her. She told them everything that had happened to her.

"You can stay with us," they said. "If you'll clean our house, cook our meals, wash and mend our clothes, we'll protect you."

But during the day while they were at work, Snow White would be alone in the house. Then she would have to be careful.

"The queen will soon find out where you are," they warned her. "Don't let anyone in." And Snow White promised them she wouldn't.

For a while the queen felt secure that she was now the most beautiful. But one day she again stood in front of her glass and said,

"Mirror, mirror, on the wall,
Who is the fairest one of all?"

And the mirror answered,

"Queen you are fairer than most, 'tis true,
But over the hills where the seven dwarfs dwell
Snow White is still alive and well,
And she's a thousand times lovelier than you."

Imagine, if you can, the queen's temper. She was dizzy with rage. The wretched girl was still alive, so the huntsman had failed her. This time she would do the job herself. She stained her face and disguised herself as a pedlar. Then she made the journey to the place where the dwarfs lived.

"Silks for sale. Ribbons and lovely laces," she called.

Snow White looked out and saw the fine things the pedlar had to sell.

"Surely it wouldn't hurt to look at the old woman's things," she thought. She unlocked the door and chose the prettiest of the laces.

"Here, let me thread it for you," the old woman offered.

Then, with fast fingers, she laced Snow White's bodice firm and tight, so tight that the girl couldn't breathe, and fell unconscious to the floor.

When the dwarfs returned that night and discovered her lying there they soon found the cause. They cut the laces and Snow White began to breathe. Then she told them about the pedlar woman.

"It was the queen, depend upon it. And she'll be back," they told her. "You must open the door to no one." And Snow White promised.

So, for a while, all was well, until the next time the queen stood in front of her mirror. Again she said,

> *"Mirror, mirror, on the wall,*
> *Who is the fairest one of all?"*

And again the mirror answered,

> *"Queen, you are fairer than most, 'tis true,*
> *But over the hills where the seven dwarfs dwell*
> *Snow White is still alive and well,*
> *And she's a thousand times lovelier than you."*

Then the queen herself could scarcely breathe for anger. This time she would have to plan more carefully. She made a poisoned comb, cleverly carved and inlaid with mother-of-pearl, certain to catch the eye. She took on a different disguise and travelled over the hills to the dwarfs' cottage.

"Come and buy," she called. "Come and buy."

Once more Snow White looked out. This time she said, "I can't open the door. I'm not allowed to."

"There's no need," said the woman. "But it doesn't hurt to look."

She held out the tantalising comb and Snow White *had* to have it. Snow White opened the door and bought it from her.

"Here, let me comb your lovely hair," said the woman.

No sooner did the comb sink into Snow White's hair than the poison set to work, and she fell senseless to the ground.

It was fortunate that the dwarfs came home quite soon and discovered the comb. Once they'd removed it she began to recover.

"This time you were lucky," they told her. "Take no more chances. Don't speak to anyone." And again Snow White promised.

When the queen returned to her castle she went straight to her mirror. Picture her fury when the mirror gave her the same answer a third time. She swore then that she would kill Snow White, even if it cost her own life. She locked herself in a secret room where she prepared a poisoned apple. It looked so tasty that it was impossible to resist, but was so deadly that one bite could kill.

This time she pretended to be a farmer's wife. She made her way to the dwarfs' cottage and knocked at the door.

Snow White looked out and said, "I'm sorry, I can't let you in."

"Don't fret," said the farmer's wife. "It makes no difference to me. Here, have an apple anyway." And she held one out.

When she saw the perfect apple, Snow White was tempted, but she shook her head. "No, I can't. I mustn't."

"What *are* you afraid of? Do you think I might poison you?" the woman laughed. "Look, I'll cut it in half and share it with you."

Now, this apple was so cunningly made that only the red half was poisoned. The old woman handed it to Snow White and started to eat the green half herself. Then Snow White felt sure it must be safe, and she took it greedily. But the moment she bit into the apple, she fell dead on the floor.

"White as snow, red as blood, black as ebony! Nothing can save you now," cried the queen.

And at long last, when she returned to the palace and stood in front of her mirror, it told her what she wanted to hear.

"Queen, you are the fairest one of all."

The queen shuddered with pleasure. Now she was satisfied, as far as a jealous heart can ever be satisfied.

When the dwarfs came home that evening they found Snow White lying dead on the ground. And this time she *was* dead. Although they tried to revive her, they couldn't do it.

For three days they mourned her and wept over her, and finally they came to bury her. But she still looked so fresh and beautiful that the thought of covering her with earth and hiding her away seemed wrong. Instead they made her a glass coffin, with her name, and an inscription saying that she was a king's daughter. They set it high on the hillside and each took turns to guard her. Even the animals and birds came and wept for her.

Time passed, and Snow White continued to look as if she were only sleeping. Then one day a young prince, travelling close by, came upon the dwarf's cottage. When he saw Snow White in her coffin he was so moved by her that he asked the dwarfs if he could take her away with him.

"Not for all the gold in the world," they said.

But the prince told them that now he had seen her, he couldn't live without her, and begged them again. At last, out of pity for him, they agreed. But as his servants lifted the coffin they stumbled and almost dropped it. The apple dislodged itself from her throat, and suddenly Snow White came back to life.

The prince told her who he was and how much he loved her. He asked her to marry him and return with him to his father's kingdom. And Snow White had only to look on him to love him too.

The marriage was arranged and everyone was invited, including Snow White's stepmother, the wicked queen.

Dressed in her finest clothes, she stood in front of her mirror and said,

"Mirror, mirror, on the wall,
Who is the fairest one of all?"

And the mirror answered,

> *"Queen you are fairer than most, 'tis true,*
> *But the new queen's even lovelier than you."*

What could it mean? The queen's heart was fit to burst with anger. First she was desperate to go, then she couldn't bear to go, then she couldn't bear *not* to go. She *had* to see who this new queen was. And when she saw it was Snow White she was fixed to the spot with fear and horror.

But red hot iron slippers had been prepared as her punishment, and the wicked woman danced in them until she was dead.

THE
LEMON PRINCESS

MARGARET MAYO

JANE RAY

ONCE, IN THE FARAWAY TIMES when toads had wings and camels could fly, there lived a king and queen who had an only son called Prince Omar; and a time came when they decided that he must do what every other prince did. He must find a beautiful girl and marry her. So Prince Omar looked for a beautiful wife, but – and it was a big but – he could not find a girl who was beautiful enough.

Then, one day, an old woman came to him and said, "My lord prince, let me tell you about a princess – an exceedingly beautiful princess – whose face has not yet been seen by the sun. She is the one you seek. She is your fate."

"How can I find her?" he asked.

"You must ride eastwards for three days and three nights," said the old woman, "and then you will come to a garden hedged around with roses, where there grows a lemon tree

that bears three ripe lemons. Pick the lemons, but then be careful and do not cut them open until you come to a place where there is plenty of water."

So the next morning Prince Omar mounted his horse and set off. He rode eastwards for three days and three nights, until he came to a garden hedged around with roses. He opened the gate and walked in. He looked all around and he found the lemon tree that had three ripe lemons. So he picked them and rode off, back the way he had come.

Now he had not gone far when he began to wonder what was inside those lemons, so he chose one, took a knife and cut it open. And there rose up from the lemon an exceedingly beautiful girl.

"Water!" she called out. "Please give me water!"

But there was no water anywhere; and the next moment the girl faded away, and she was gone.

Prince Omar was sad. But the thing was done, and there was no going back. So on he rode.

It was not long, however, before he began to wonder about the other two lemons and whether there were girls in them also. So he chose another one, took his knife and cut it open. And there rose up from the lemon a girl who was even more beautiful than the first, and she called out, "Water! Please give me water!"

But again there was no water anywhere; and the girl faded away, and she was gone.

"I see now that I must take great care of my third lemon," said the prince. And on he rode.

After a while he came to a river, and, remembering the old woman's advice, he took the third lemon and cut it open. And there rose up a girl who was even more beautiful than the two who had come before – eyes gentle as the moon, skin pale as ivory, and hair long, shiny black and soft as silk. And she too called out, "Water! Please give me water!"

Well, Prince Omar was so anxious not to lose this beautiful girl that he took hold of her and dropped her straight into the river. Just like that. And she drank the clear, fresh water until she was satisfied, and then she climbed out, all naked as she was.

The prince took off his cloak and wrapped it round her. "My beautiful Lemon Princess, you, and you alone, shall be my bride," he said. "But, before I take you to the palace, I must go and fetch some fine clothes for you to wear and a horse for you to ride."

"Then I shall hide in this tall poplar tree, until you return," said the Lemon Princess. And with that she called out, "Bend down, tall tree! Bend down!"

Immediately the tree bent down and she seated herself on the topmost branch, and the tree stood tall again. And then Prince Omar rode off.

Time comes, time goes, and the Lemon Princess sat high in the tree and waited. After a while, a servant girl – an ugly girl, with mean eyes, tangled hair and rough skin – came to fill her water jar at the river. As she bent down, she saw the face of the beautiful Lemon Princess reflected in the clear water.

"There – see how beautiful I am!" she cried. "I always knew I was far too beautiful to be a servant!"

Then she heard someone laugh and a voice call out, "Look up, not down!"

So the servant girl looked up, and when she saw the Lemon Princess sitting at the very top of the poplar tree, she said, "What are you doing up there in that tall tree?"

The Lemon Princess answered, "I am waiting for my bridegroom, the royal prince, to return with fine clothes for me to wear and a horse for me to ride."

Then the servant girl thought some wicked thoughts and she said, "O lady, lovely lady, let me come up and talk to you and help pass the weary hours while you wait."

The Lemon Princess was lonely, so she said, "Bend down, tall tree! Bend down!" And the tree bent down, and the servant girl was soon up amongst the topmost branches.

"O lady, lovely lady," said the servant girl, "who are you with your magic powers? Are you human? Or are you a peri maiden from the land of enchantment?"

The Lemon Princess answered, "I was once a peri maiden, but now I have chosen to enter the world of humans and to become the Lemon Princess."

"O lady, lovely lady, let me comb your long black hair." And the servant girl began to comb the Lemon Princess's hair and then – and then she found a hairpin stuck deep in her long black hair.

"O lady, lovely lady, what is this?" she asked.

"It is my talisman," said the Lemon Princess. "Do not touch it."

Immediately the servant girl pulled out the hairpin, and *whir-r-r-r!* the Lemon Princess changed into a white dove, fluttered her wings and flew up and away.

Then the servant girl took off her own clothes, threw them into the river below and they floated away. Then she wrapped the prince's cloak around her and waited.

Now when Prince Omar returned and saw the ugly servant girl in the poplar tree, he was amazed.

"What has happened?" he cried. "You have changed. Your skin is rough and dry."

"It was the sun, my lord," she said. "The scorching sun burnt it."

"But your lips? Your lips that were soft as rosebuds. What about them?"

"It was the wind, my lord," she said. "The hot dry wind cracked them."

"But your eyes that were so large and gentle?"

"It was the tears, my lord," she said. "The tears I wept because I thought you would never return have made them red and swollen."

"But your hair that was soft as silk?"

"It was the black crow, my lord," she said. "The black crow tried to build a nest in my hair and tangled it and made it rough."

Then the ugly servant girl climbed down from the tree and said, "Time is a great healer, my lord. Soon I shall be as I was before."

And Prince Omar believed her. He gave her beautiful clothes to wear – bag trousers, blue as the summer sky, a white silk blouse embroidered with pearls, a jacket of gold thread, gold slippers, a gold head-dress and gold bangles. And then, together, they rode off to the palace.

Well, when Prince Omar took the servant girl to meet the king and queen, they saw at once how ugly she was and they said, "*This* is your chosen bride! Surely not!"

"I have given her my word," said the prince. "And in forty days our marriage will be celebrated."

Now there was a garden around the king's palace, and every morning a white dove came and sat upon a sandalwood tree and sang. Every day Prince Omar came and stood beneath the tree and listened, and every day he said, "How sad is the song that the white dove sings!"

As soon as the servant girl noticed this, she went to the gardener and said, "The prince commands you to catch the white dove that sings the sad song in the sandalwood tree and kill it and bury it deep in the ground."

And the gardener killed the bird and buried it.

But the next day, at the very place where the dove was buried, there sprang up a great cypress tree, and the wind came and sighed in its branches.

When Prince Omar saw the tree he was astonished. "What wonder is this!" he said. "A cypress where no tree stood before." And when he heard the wind sighing, he said, "How sad is the sound of the wind in its branches!"

Then the servant girl went to the gardener and said, "The prince commands you to cut down the cypress tree and make from its wood a cradle for the son which one day I shall give him. Take any wood that remains and burn it."

And the gardener cut down the tree, and the palace carpenters cut the wood into planks and made a cradle. Then the gardener gathered all the wood that remained and built a fire. He was just going to throw the last small branch on to the flames, when the prince's old nurse went by and asked him for some firewood, so he gave her the small branch from the cypress tree.

Now the old nurse put the branch down beside the fireplace in her house, while she went off to market. The moment she shut the door, the branch shivered all over and – well! – it changed into a girl. An exceedingly beautiful girl. The Lemon Princess herself.

At once she set to work. She swept the floor. She washed the dishes. She peeled vegetables and cooked a meal. And then she hid behind a door.

When the old nurse returned, she *was* surprised. "Who has done all this?" she said. "A human or one of the peri kind?"

Then the Lemon Princess came out from her hiding place and she said, "I cleaned and I cooked for you, and now, I ask you, will you do something for me? Go to Prince Omar and tell him that there lives in your house a girl who can make fine carpets, and if he will give you silk threads, she will make for him the finest carpet ever seen."

The old nurse went and spoke to the prince, and he ordered that she should be given silk threads and anything else that was needed.

So then the Lemon Princess set to work on her carpet.

Time comes, time goes. The day came when Prince Omar was to marry the wicked servant girl. She had not changed: she was as ugly as ever. But the prince said to himself,

"Surely she *is* the Lemon Princess – the one who is my fate. Besides, I have given my word, and so I must marry her."

But early in the morning of that very day, the old nurse brought the finished carpet to the prince and said, "My lord prince, here is a wedding gift!"

Prince Omar unrolled the carpet and looked; and there was a picture of a garden hedged all around with roses, and in the centre of the garden was a portrait of the Lemon Princess.

"Who made this carpet?" asked the prince.

"A girl who lives with me," she answered.

"Bring her to me," he said.

So the Lemon Princess came to the palace; and the moment Prince Omar saw her, he knew her.

"Truly," he said, "you alone are my beautiful Lemon Princess – my fate – the one who must be my bride. But, tell me, where have you been? What happened to you these long and weary days?"

Then the Lemon Princess told him about the wicked servant girl and all her evil deeds. And the prince was angry and sent his guards to find the servant girl. But as soon as she heard that she had been discovered, she was up and off, with the guards at her heels. And she kept running until she was over the border and into the next kingdom. Some say she's running still!

But then, at last, there was a wedding, and Prince Omar married the beautiful Lemon Princess. And for seven days and seven nights the pipes were played, the drums rolled and there was feasting, dancing and great merriment.

THE
LITTLE MERMAID

ANDREW MATTHEWS

ALAN SNOW

DOWN IN THE BLUEST DEEPS of the ocean grew a great forest of sea plants. When the tides changed, the plants swayed like trees in the wind, and bright fish flickered between their branches. In the middle of the underwater forest stood the castle of the Sea King. Its walls were made of pink coral and its roof was made of shells.

The Sea King's wife had died years before and he lived in the palace with his old mother, who helped him to bring up his six daughters. They were all beautiful, but the youngest was the loveliest, with skin as soft as petals and eyes as blue as the ocean. Like all the sea people, she had a fish-tail instead of legs.

The little mermaid loved to hear her grandmother tell stories about the world of humans, far above the waves.

"Up there, the forests are green," said Grandmother. "Birds fly about singing pretty songs and wonderful-smelling flowers grow everywhere."

"When can I visit the world of humans?" asked the little mermaid.

"Not yet!" came the reply. "When you're fifteen, you will
come of age and then you can swim up and sit on rocks
in the moonlight. You'll see ships, and forests and towns."

"But I won't be fifteen for five years!" cried the little
mermaid.

"Then you must learn to be patient, dear child,"
Grandmother told her.

One by one, the little mermaid's sisters came of age and
visited the surface. When they talked about the things they
had seen, the little mermaid felt that she couldn't wait to see
it all for herself.

"I wish I were fifteen *now*!" she complained. "I'm sure I'm
going to love the world up there."

"Oh, it's quite interesting at first," said her sisters, "but
you'll soon grow tired of it, as we did. Being underwater is
best, though humans don't understand that. Why, if they
spent more than a minute or so below the surface, they
would drown – poor things!"

At long last, the little mermaid's fifteenth birthday
arrived. She was dressed in a wreath of pearls. She kissed
her family goodbye and swam up to the surface,
excited about what she would find.

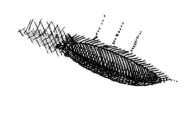

The first thing she saw of the upper world was a sunset that turned the clouds red and gold. Nearby was a big ship with three masts. It was still because there was no wind to push it along. The ship's decks were lined with coloured lamps and the little mermaid could hear laughter and singing. Curious, she swam closer. A friendly wave lifted her so that she could see in through the cabin windows.

She saw many finely dressed people, and the most handsome was a young prince. It was his sixteenth birthday and everybody was celebrating. The sailors danced on the deck, and when the prince came out of his cabin to watch, hundreds of rockets were fired off into the air. They burst in fiery colours that were reflected in the sea and in the prince's eyes.

The little mermaid stared and stared at the prince. Long after the birthday party ended and the prince went back into his cabin, she waited, hoping to see him again.

At midnight, a wind blew up and filled the ship's sails. It raised huge waves and made dark clouds gather. Lightning crackled and the wind howled. The ship raced between waves as high as black mountains. The little mermaid followed, thinking that the storm was great fun.

Then a great wave crashed down on the ship. It snapped the
masts and tipped the ship over on its side, so that water
rushed in.

As the ship sank, the little mermaid remembered that
humans could not live under water. If she did not help the
handsome young prince, he would drown. Through the
screeching wind and lashing waves she searched for him,
dodging the heavy planks and beams that floated away from
the sinking ship. A bolt of lightning lit up the sky and the
sea, and the little mermaid saw the prince. He had
grown so weak that he could hardly swim.

His eyes closed and he began to slip under. The little
mermaid caught him in her arms and kept his head above

the water. She held him fast all night, and though her arms ached with his weight, she would not let him go.

At dawn, they drifted into a bay where orange and lemon trees grew. Near the shore was a tall white temple. The little mermaid swam across the bay and laid the prince safely on a stretch of soft yellow sand. She kissed his forehead, then swam back out to sea until she came to a rock where she could hide and watch without being seen.

Bells rang and a crowd of young girls came out of the temple. One of them ran down to the beach. She shouted with surprise as she almost stumbled over the prince. The sound of her cry woke him. He opened his eyes and smiled at the girl. Other girls came running and together they carried the prince inside the temple.

The little mermaid was glad the prince was safe, but she felt sad as she dived down and returned to her father's palace. She was so sad that when her sisters asked what she had seen, she said nothing.

Day after day she swam back to the bay, thinking she might catch sight of the prince, but he was never there, and day after day her heart grew heavier. At last, her sadness was too great for her to carry alone and she told her sisters what had happened.

"Come with us," they said.

Arm in arm, the sisters swam to the surface and showed
the little mermaid the palace where the prince lived. It
stood beside a river that ran into the sea, and a great marble
staircase came down to the water where one of the prince's
ships was moored. The little mermaid visited the palace
every morning and every evening, swimming up the river
to get as close as she dared. Many times she saw the prince
strolling in the moonlight; many times she followed his
boat when he went sailing; each time she saw the prince,
the little mermaid loved him more.

"Put him out of your mind!" her sisters advised. "Humans
never fall in love with mermaids. They think our beautiful

tails are ugly. Of course, the prince might love you if your tail turned into legs, but without magic that would be impossible."

When she heard this, the little mermaid knew that the only person who could help her was the sea witch. She swam away from her father's palace, past whirlpools and bubbling mud until she reached the grey sand desert where the witch lived, in a house made from the bones of drowned sailors.

The sea witch was in her garden, letting her pet eels take food from her mouth. When she caught sight of the little mermaid, the witch smiled, showing the barnacles that grew on her teeth.

"I know all about you and your prince, and I know what you want," she said. "If I make you a magic potion and you swim ashore and drink it before the sun rises, your tail will split in two and turn into legs. But it will be very painful.

You'll be able to walk and dance beautifully, but it will feel as though you were treading on razors. Are you willing to suffer all this to try and win the prince's love?"

"Yes," whispered the little mermaid.

"But remember," said the witch, "once you have legs, you can never be a mermaid again. And if your precious prince should marry someone else, then the morning after he has married, your heart will break and you will turn into foam on the water."

"I understand," said the little mermaid.

"And the price of my potion is . . . your voice!" the witch cackled.

"But how can I tell the prince I love him without my voice?" pleaded the little mermaid.

"Make up your mind quickly!" snapped the witch. "Time is growing short!"

The little mermaid nodded her agreement. The sea witch put her hand over the mermaid's mouth and pulled out her voice by magic; then she brewed the magic potion in a black cauldron. When it was ready, she poured the potion into a tiny bottle and gave it to the little mermaid.

"You'd better hurry," said the witch. "In the world above, the sky is already getting light."

The little mermaid swam to the surface as fast as she could. By the time she reached the prince's palace, the edge of the sun was showing above the horizon. She dragged herself on to the bottom of the marble staircase and drank the witch's potion. It burned her throat; she felt as though a sword were cutting her in half and the pain made her faint.

She woke when the sun shone over the sea, and there was the prince, standing at the top of the stairs, gazing at her in amazement. She blushed and looked down – and saw two pretty white legs where her tail had been.

The prince asked who she was and where she was from, but the little mermaid had no voice to answer him. She could only gaze at him sadly with her deep blue eyes. He took her hand and led her to the palace, and though every step felt as though she were walking on needles and knives, she walked gracefully and smiled whenever the prince looked at her.

Inside the palace, the mermaid was dressed in a silk gown. The prince's parents declared that she was the greatest beauty in the palace and insisted that she must live with them as long as she liked.

At dinner that evening, when the royal musicians played, the little mermaid rose from her place and danced. Sharp pains darted through her feet, but she ignored them, moving as lightly as a feather in the breeze. She stared at the prince, trying to tell him with her eyes and her dance how much she loved him. Though her dancing pleased him, he did not guess what it meant.

As the days went by, the prince seemed to grow more and more fond of the silent stranger he had found and the little mermaid's heart filled with hope, until one morning, when she and the prince were walking together in the palace garden.

"My dear, I've come to love you as a friend," he sighed. "And I badly need a friend I can talk to. Tomorrow I must go on a voyage to another kingdom, to meet a beautiful princess. My parents insist that I must marry her, but how can I? You see, a few months ago I was shipwrecked. The sea washed me up near a temple and a young girl from the temple found me and saved my life. That was the only time I met her, and I don't even know her name, but I know she is the only girl I could ever love."

"He doesn't know I saved him," the little mermaid thought sadly. "He doesn't know that I was the one who carried him through the waves to the temple, where he met the girl he loves more than me."

"Don't look so sad, my friend," smiled the prince. "I want you to sail with me and cheer me up with your dancing."

It took a day and a night for the prince's ship to reach harbour. The king and queen and crowds of cheering people greeted the prince, but there was no sign of the princess.

"She must have been delayed," the king explained. "I've had her educated in a temple. It's rather a long way from here and—"

A fanfare of trumpets interrupted him. The cheering crowds parted and the princess appeared.

"Why, it's her!" cried the prince. "She's the girl from the temple who saved me when I was lying nearly dead on the shore! I can't believe it! We must be married at once!"

That afternoon, the church bells rang and the crowds cheered even more loudly as the prince and princess were married in a grand cathedral. The little mermaid, in a dress of silk and gold, stood close to the prince throughout the wedding, but she saw and heard nothing. She kept on remembering the sea witch's words –

"And if your precious prince should marry someone else, then the morning after he has married, your heart will break and you will turn into foam on the water."

In the evening, the bride and groom set sail for the prince's home. When it grew dark, lamps were lit and the sailors danced. The little mermaid danced with them, dancing for her prince one last time, though he was too busy looking at his lovely wife to notice.

It was past midnight before the dancing ended. After everyone had gone to bed, the little mermaid stayed on deck, staring down into the dark water. She thought of her father's palace below the waves and how sad it was that she would never return there. Suddenly, she saw the heads of her sisters rise out of the sea. Their hair had been cut short.

"We gave our hair to the sea witch," they said. "In exchange, she gave us this magic knife. Take it and kill the prince, and you will not die. Your tail will grow again and you can dive down into the sea with us! Hurry, that red streak in the sky means the sun will rise soon! Kill the prince and come back to us!"

The little mermaid took the knife from her sisters and hurried to the prince's cabin; but when she opened the door and saw him lying asleep, whispering his bride's name, her heart broke. She rushed back on deck and hurled the knife far out into the waves that were blood-red with the light of dawn. The little mermaid threw herself into the sea and felt her body dissolving into foam.

"I shall turn into water," she thought. "The water will rise up into clouds and fly over the land and fall as rain. The rain will run into rivers and flow back to the sea, over and over again. Wherever my prince is, on land, or sea, or in the air, I shall be with him . . ."

Then the foam on the water vanished, and there
was nothing to be seen except the great ship riding
gently through the waves, and the white sea birds
circling overhead.

SWAN LAKE

GERALDINE MCCAUGHREAN

ANGELA BARRETT

A PRINCE'S BIRTHDAY! Days of celebration! Feasting! Presents! Dancing! Heralds carried the invitation far and wide: "Come to the Royal Castle tomorrow, for Prince Siegfried is twenty-one years old and will soon take his rightful place as king!"

Already the castle gardens were crowded with people from the village, all come to wish Prince Siegfried happy birthday with flowers and dancing.

"There! There he is!" they cheered. "Oh, isn't he handsome! Imagine being *married* to someone as handsome as that!"

"I wonder who he'll choose for a wife!"

"The prince? Marry? He'd sooner go hunting with his friends."

It was true. Siegfried's mother, the queen, was quite upset

about it. She knew how much he liked hunting: she even gave him a crossbow for his birthday present. But she also knew it was time for the prince to be choosing a wife, marrying, having sons and daughters of his own. She often spoke to him about it. She even invited beautiful princesses to the castle. But Siegfried never paid them any attention. He just rode off into the forests with his friends, and left the princesses taking tea with the queen. "*Really*, Siegfried, parties are all very well," his mother said, "but you must start taking life more seriously. You must choose a bride. Tell him, Wolfgang. You're his teacher. Tell him how important it is!" Away went the queen, but the prince had hardly heard a word she said. He was too busy admiring his new crossbow.

"Your excellent mother is quite right, young man," said old Wolfgang sternly. "There are some things far more important than parties. Be a good boy. Choose a nice, pretty girl at the ball tomorrow and settle down."

But Siegfried had hardly heard a word his teacher said. He was too busy watching a skein of swans flying across the sky. "Swans! Come on everybody! Let's practise our shooting!" cried the prince. "With any luck there'll be something better than princesses at the ball tomorrow: there'll be roast swan!"

All the young huntsmen set off together for the wood. But in among the trees, searching for the swans, they were soon separated. Siegfried found himself alone beside a lake. The flock of swans had landed on the water and were swimming towards the bank. They paddled ashore on their large black feet, all the little cygnets flurrying out together. Last to come was the whitest swan of all, wearing – could it be? – *a golden crown.* Siegfried laid an arrow to his bow.

That was when he saw it: that most wonderful of sights. The milk-white swan spread its wide wings, stretched its long neck high in the air, and the feathers, the great black feet, the orange beak, the wings – all but the crown – melted away like snow.

There stood a beautiful woman, lifting a gown of white above her knees as she waded ashore. Next moment all the other swans were transformed into young women, the cygnets into little children. Siegfried's crossbow dropped from his hands and the noise startled them.

"Don't be afraid!" he exclaimed in a whisper. "Am I dreaming? Tell me, who are you?"

The girl in the crown looked about her with shining black eyes.

"It's dangerous. Von Rothbart will be watching. He's always watching!" But Siegfried would not leave until he had heard her whole unhappy story.

The swan-maiden's name was Odette – Princess Odette – her kingdom a land far, far away. She and her ladies-in-waiting, even their little children, were prisoners of a terrible magic. And who but the sorcerer von Rothbart could have cast a spell so wicked over such a princess? She and all the swan-maidens were doomed by a terrible curse:

> *Flap and fly*
> *In the weary sky;*
> *By day a swan*
> *With feathers wan;*
> *Only at night*
> *The lovely sight*
> *Which once I swore*
> *Would never more*
> *Offend my sight*
> *With goodness bright.*
> *The world will soon forget*
> *Princess Odette!*

Even at night, when they wore human shape, the evil von Rothbart kept watch over his prisoners, disguised as an owl, yellow eyes watching, watching, watching.

"Can nothing save you?" cried Prince Siegfried. All night he had sat and listened to her story.

"Nothing but love," she said sadly.

"Oh, then you're saved!" It was true: Siegfried had loved
her ever since the first moment he saw her black eyes shine.
All night his love had been growing. "*I* love you!" he
exclaimed.

"Oh, but you would have to swear to love me for ever.
Nothing less can break the spell!"

"I'll do it!" he cried, without a moment's thought.

But daylight was already creeping through the trees.
Odette pulled away from him, drawn by magic back into
the lake. Her arms began to stiffen into fronded wings.

"Come to the castle tomorrow!" called Siegfried. "To the
birthday ball! Come, and I'll choose you for my wife!"

Somewhere an owl hooted, a terrible, dismal sound.
A milk-white swan gliding out over the lake nodded her
lovely head.

"Does he think he can break my spell so easily?" Von
Rothbart hooted with laughter, and his daughter laughed too.

His spiteful, spoiled, ugly daughter Odile laughed a
quacking laugh. "So you won't let her marry him?" Odile
had wanted the handsome prince for many years and hated
Odette for winning his love.

"No, no. *You* shall have that honour," said the sorcerer.
"Tonight I shall mask you in magic and dress you in disguise.
I'll give you the face of Odette. You shall dance the night
away while Siegfried swears away his love for ever!" Again
he hooted with laughter, just like an owl.

That night, at the castle, the air glistened with ribbons and silk. Princesses with hair of yellow and black and brown arrived in coaches of gold and silver and glass to smile at Prince Siegfried and wish him happy birthday. (What they really wished was to marry him, of course.)

"Meet Princess Zoë," said the queen.

"Meet Princess Chloë.

"Meet Princess Clothilda.

"Meet Princess Matilda.

"Meet Princess Mariana," said the queen. "Meet Princess Tatiana!"

But Siegfried only looked over their shoulders, watching the door, waiting for Odette to arrive.

There! A woman dressed all in scarlet swept into the ballroom, lifted her veil and – yes! There were Odette's black eyes, Odette's white skin, Odette's sweet red mouth. Siegfried rushed to take her in his arms, and the dancing began. Apart from the princesses, the guests were amazed and delighted to see such a change in the prince.

But he should have looked more deeply into those black eyes.

"Now you may swear that you love me," said Odile.

"Oh, I do! I swear it!"

With a noise like a heart breaking, a pane of glass broke
in the tall castle windows. There, battering against the
glass with wide, white wings, pecking at the glass with
an orange beak, kicking at the glass with large black feet,
was a milk-white swan.

Odette flung herself against the window so hard that
it burst open. But a guest at the party, a man with large yellow
eyes, slammed the window shut again with a hooting laugh.

"For ever and a day. Swear!" said Odile.

"For ever and a day!" vowed Siegfried.

"And so you have chosen your wife," declared von
Rothbart. "Sworn undying love to my dear daughter, Odile."

"*Odile?*"

"Congratulations, my dear son-in-law."

Siegfried looked up then and caught sight of von
Rothbart and, beyond him, clamouring against the glass,
the ragged, haggard shape of a swan.

"Come, Odile!" said her father. "We have what we came for!"

"Never!" cried the prince. But as he drew his sword and rushed towards the sorcerer, the room filled with smoke and thunder.

"What? Do you think a puny sword can destroy an evil the like of mine?" cried von Rothbart.

A howling wind blew open all the windows. And away across a black and thundery sky, a swan was swept by the magician's stormy laughter, over the treetops, towards the lake.

The day ended. The sun sank and returned Odette to human shape. But it took with it all her hopes and dreams. When her friends saw her coming through the woods, her hair wild, her gown torn, her hands bruised with banging on the window's glass, they knew that Siegfried had not broken the spell. They were doomed for ever to be swans by day, maidens by night.

"He forgot me! He forgot me! So soon he forgot me! He danced with Odile! He swore to love Odile! He chose Odile to be his wife!" She rushed past them to the shore of the lake and was about to throw herself into the water.

"Wait! Princess! What are you doing?" The swan-maidens thought she must have forgotten that she was not a swimming swan.

"I can't wait! If I'm going to drown myself, I must do it while I'm in human form!"

"Drown yourself? No!" Her friends pulled her away from the water, but they could do nothing to comfort her.

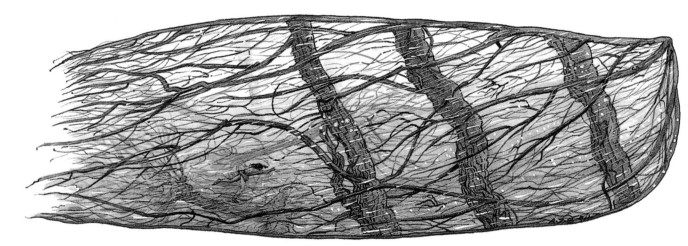

"I'll find her! I'll explain! I was tricked! My vow means nothing!" wailed Prince Siegfried as he raced through the rainy woods.

Rain, sleet, snow. The wind howled and the trees crashed down around him. Von Rothbart's magic was at work, trying to stop the prince from reaching Odette. But he fought his way past the lashing branches, he bent his head into the driving rain and he stumbled on towards the lake. "Odette! I'm sorry! Odette! Forgive me!"

She heard him coming. She would have run away, but he

caught her up in his arms. "Forgive me, Odette! I was tricked by the villain Rothbart. He tricked me with magic. He blinded me, so that I couldn't see you until it was too late. But he can't blind me to the truth. It's you I love, not Odile. It's you I shall love for ever!"

She forgave him, of course she did. But she did so sadly, with eyes full of tears. "I love you too, Siegfried, but nothing can undo what's done. Your promise is made, and I and my ladies will be prisoners for ever, swans by day and women by night. And Odile shall be your queen."

"That's right!" cried von Rothbart appearing in a clap of thunder, with a laugh like lightning. "My prisoners always, in a land where my daughter is queen! You! Swan-maidens! Dawn is coming. Get back to your lake now. Preen your white feathers and waddle on your black feet, and eat weed as I taught you!"

The swan-maidens fled, sobbing with terror.

But Odette clung to the prince. "Oh, Siegfried! I wish you had shot me with your crossbow that first time you saw me! Life will be nothing without you!"

"You're right," whispered Siegfried. "But why live apart when we can die together?"

Von Rothbart heard them. The words struck terror into his wicked soul, "No!" he begged. "NO!"

But they did not hear him. Princess Odette and Prince Siegfried were looking into each other's eyes as they plunged into the lake and the chilly waters closed over them.

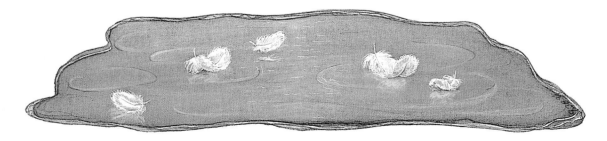

In that moment, all von Rothbart's magic burst inside him, scalding, freezing, poisonous, deadly. He fell dead on the spot.

The swan-maidens, and their frightened little cygnets, found themselves ankle-deep in water, surrounded by fallen feathers.

The spell was broken.

Dawn rose over the lake: sunlight danced on the water.
And there, in a magical world of light, somewhere between
Earth and Sky, Prince Siegfried and Princess Odette danced
too, together for ever, for ever dancing for joy. Their love
had been far too great for Death to hold prisoner. They
simply slipped out of its grasp, to live together in a world
of never-ending happiness.

THE TWELVE DANCING PRINCESSES

Saviour Pirotta

Emma Chichester Clark

THERE WAS ONCE A KING who had twelve beautiful daughters. He was very proud of them and kept a close eye on them all day long. At bedtime he locked them all in one vast bedroom with twelve beds, to make sure they were safe. In the morning he unlocked their door himself, with a golden key he kept on a chain around his neck.

One morning, when the king unlocked the bedroom door, he saw that the princesses' satin shoes had been danced to pieces. No one knew how the princesses had managed to escape from their room, nor who they had danced with. And they weren't saying, no matter how much their father pleaded with them or scolded them.

The same thing happened the next night and the night after that. The mystery bothered the king and,

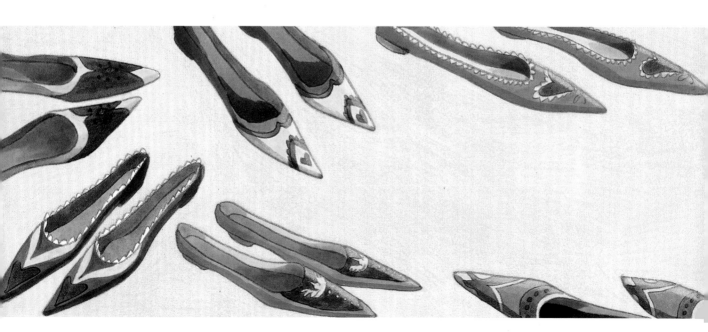

when it seemed that the princesses would not stop sneaking out of the palace, he decided to solve it once and for all.

He sent out a proclamation, inviting all the young men of the land to discover the princesses' secret. Anyone who did, could choose one of the king's daughters to marry and would inherit the kingdom. But anyone who tried and failed three nights in a row would lose his head on the executioner's block.

Many a dashing young prince accepted the challenge. In turn, each was given a sumptuous supper and at bedtime was shown to a chamber adjoining the princesses' bedroom. The door between the two rooms was kept open, so the prince could observe the king's daughters.

But, in turn, each prince fell asleep at his task and in the morning, the princesses' shoes were found tattered and torn. Many princes lost their lives and the princesses' secret remained just that: a secret.

Now it so happened that a poor soldier found himself on the outskirts of the city where the king lived. He had been wounded in battle and discharged with a medal but he had no idea where he was to settle, or how he was going to earn a living. By chance he met a kind old woman who, seeing the pain and weariness in his face, said, "Where are you going, my son?"

And he replied jokingly, "I have no idea, but I might try and discover where the king's daughters dance at night, then I could become king."

"In that case," said the woman, who was really a kind witch, "do not drink the wine that the princesses offer you, because it will have a sleeping potion in it. Just pretend to be fast asleep and, when the princesses go out, follow them closely." She handed the soldier a cloak. "Put this on your shoulders," she whispered, "and it will make you invisible; that way you can observe the girls without being seen yourself."

The soldier thanked the old woman and hurried to the palace. Even though he looked poor, he was as well-received as the princes had been. He was given a delicious supper and shown to the room adjoining the princesses' chamber. As he was about to get into bed, the eldest offered him a goblet of wine. The soldier pretended to drink it but, when the girl wasn't looking, he emptied the goblet into the chamberpot under the bed. Then he lay down, yawned and began to snore loudly.

"The fool is asleep already," said the eldest princess. "The journey to the palace must have tired him out."

"Poor wretch," said another, "he is sure to

lose his head in three days' time."

Then the twelve princesses put on silk party dresses, jewelled crowns and satin dancing shoes. Just before leaving, they took one last look at the soldier to make sure he was still fast asleep.

"Are you certain he will not wake up before the morning?" asked the youngest princess. "I have an awful feeling that something dreadful is about to happen."

"You are always in dread of one thing or another," mocked the eldest. "There is nothing to fear." Then she knocked on one of the beds and it sank into the floor, revealing a secret staircase. The princesses descended through the opening, one after another.

The soldier, who had secretly been watching everything from his bed, put on his magic cloak and quickly followed them. It was dark in the passage and, halfway down the stairs, he trod on the youngest princess's gown.

"We're being followed," cried the princess. "Someone has just tugged on my gown."

"Don't be foolish," said the eldest sister. "You must have caught your dress on a nail."

At the bottom of the stairs was a garden full of silvery trees, which shone brightly and filled the place with light. The soldier, unable to help himself, reached out and snapped off a twig.

"Did none of you hear that noise?" said the youngest princess. "I am sure we are not alone."

"It is only our princes who wait for us," scolded the eldest princess. She led the way into a second garden, where the trees were made of gold, and then on to a third where the trees were laden with diamonds.

In each garden, the soldier broke off a twig and the youngest princess gasped at the sound, but she did not say

anything else to her sisters for fear of being ridiculed.

At last the princesses reached the shores of a lake.
The soldier, coming up behind them, saw twelve handsome
princes, each one sitting in a boat with a golden lion's
head on the prow. Every princess got into a boat, and the
soldier – fearing he might be left behind – hopped in
with the youngest.

"The boat seems very heavy tonight," said her prince
as he rowed.

"It must be the summer heat," said the youngest princess.
"I feel a bit tired and listless too."

Soon all twelve boats were moored outside a palace
on the other side of the lake. Each prince took his princess
by the hand and led her up a flight of marble steps into
a beautiful ballroom. There, the happy couples danced
to the sound of music, the princesses whirling gaily
around in their satin shoes. The soldier danced too,
and every time he brushed past the youngest princess,
she would stifle a gasp and say: "I can feel a presence in
this room; I am sure of it."